Magical Mayhem

Book One

To Prevent World Peace

Emily Martha Sorensen

To Prevent World Peace

To Frederik Vendelin,

longtime fan of the comic,
reader of my other books,
and Patreon supporter.

Chapter 1
The Future

It was a microphone, shaped like a flower. A tall woman stood behind it, elegant and emanating authority, for all the fact that she was barely eighteen.

She lifted her chin, surveying the crowd before her. A sea of teenagers and children watched breathlessly, eager for her guidance. Anxious to hear what they should do.

"The villains," the woman said, "are dead."

A sigh went out across the whole audience. A sigh of relief, of pleasure, of anticipation.

"The Olympians are slain," the woman continued. "The Deathwaves have disbanded. The invaders from other worlds have all fled. For the first time since magic came to us in order to save this world, we have world peace."

A murmur of excitement danced across the crowd. Almost all of them were children and teenagers. Almost all of them were female. A great many of them wore colorful costumes, were surrounded by animal critters, or had magical glows or sparkles around them.

"But!" the woman snapped sharply, bringing their attention back to her.

The crowd stilled. Murmuring stopped, and eyes fastened back onto the speaker.

"But," the woman said more softly, "our problems are not over. For now there are those saying that where there is power, there can be both good and evil. Now there are those saying that we are no longer needed. That our magic should be set down. That we should renounce our powers and join the ranks of mediocrity."

Her voice rose sharply.

"Is this right?!"

"NO!" the crowd shouted.

"Is this fair?!"

"*NO!*" the crowd shouted.

"Will we do this?!"

"*NO!!*" the crowd screamed.

Teenage girls clenched fists in outrage. Middle school girls looked hurt. Younger girls looked like they had no idea what was going on, but they enjoyed the opportunity to yell.

The woman at the podium held up her hand.

Silence fell.

A few little girls shouted "*No!*" from the crowd, just in case there was about to be another question.

The speaker waited for a moment, and then she answered.

"No," she said quietly. "We created this peace, and we are the only ones who can defend it. Without us, everything we've built will crumble, wither and die. So even now, we must continue to fight — to protect world peace!"

"World peace! World peace! World peace!" the crowd shouted. "World peace! World peace! World peace!"

One little girl near the front looked baffled. She stared up at a slender teenage girl beside her, probably an older sister. Then the small child's face brightened, and she started chanting along with the rest of the crowd. "Would peas! Would peas! Would peas!"

"Magical girls have protected our world for four and a half generations!" the woman shouted from the podium. The microphone shaped like a flower trembled. "And yet now, the politicians say we are no longer needed! We were *given* this magic to protect the world! We were *given* this magic to save it! *We must do that!*"

"World peace! World peace! World peace!"

The Future

Gigantic feathered wings sprouted from the speaker's back, and she zoomed up into the air, presiding over the fervor of the crowd. Then, just as the screaming reached its peak, she plunged down and soared off into the distance.

An alarmed-looking man scrambled up to the stage and grabbed the microphone. "A big thank you to our chairwoman — Avenging Angel!"

"World peace! World peace! World peace!" the crowd chanted. "World peace! World peace! World peace!"

There was no "Would peas" any longer. The little girl near the front had fallen asleep, sucking her thumb.

The blonde-haired woman with the glorious feathered wings landed. Waiting for her was another woman, dark-skinned and bat-winged. This woman wore a crimson blouse and a long, layered skirt that looked like it had once been fluffy, but had morphed into shreds.

"Terrific, Kendra," the brown-skinned woman said. She put her hands on her hips. "That was not what you were supposed to say. Presidente Santos will be furious."

"Presidente Santos can do what she likes," the blonde-haired woman said. Feathers glowed around her as she detransformed back into ordinary attire: a T-shirt and jeans with a butterfly patch on each of the back pockets. "It had to be said, and you know it."

"I do *not* know that," her friend snapped. "We're magical girls, not governments. Who elected us to decide the world's fate?"

"Magic itself did," Kendra said. "We were chosen as the most pure in heart. Who else is so qualified?"

The brown-skinned woman looked troubled.

"Do you disagree?" Kendra demanded, folding her arms.

"No . . ." her friend said slowly. "But I do believe in democracy. Not . . . whatever you're doing. You're the reason governments are getting scared of magical girls."

"They were always scared of us," Kendra said scornfully. "Why do you think there's so much pressure to relinquish powers in early teenage years? Because children can be *controlled*."

"I know that that's a touchy subject for you," the brown-skinned woman said slowly. "I know you think all magical girls should keep their powers until magic decides to leave because they're unworthy or too old. But Kendra, the only reason Presidente Santos allowed you to call that press conference in the first place was because you agreed to . . ."

"I'll agree to anything," Kendra cut her off, "if it's a necessary step to reaching my goals. That doesn't mean I'll *do* it. Listen."

In the background, the chanting was growing louder and louder and louder. Other flying magical girls were now filling the sky. "World peace! World peace! World peace!"

"What did you *do?*" the brown-skinned woman asked in horror.

"You might ask, rather," Kendra said in satisfaction, "what did Namikaze do when I gave her the signal?"

"What did *she* do?!"

Kendra smiled. "They're going to the border. For a . . . peaceful demonstration against Brazil's demands that we give up our powers. Such an unimaginably stupid thing for them to do."

"You've probably just started a war, you know."

The smirk fell from Kendra's face. "I know."

"And you really think that risk was worth it?" her friend snapped.

"If there's a war, we'll win," Kendra shrugged.

"That wasn't my question."

Kendra sighed heavily. She reached out and pushed a stray hair back behind her ear. "Flo, you know *someone* has to rule the world. And the only people pure enough to do it are the magical girls. If it takes a war to stop all wars forever, that's what we'll do."

The myriad future wars, the multitudes of deaths and chaos, smashed through Chronos's mind and jerked her awake. She sat bolt upright, gasping.

The Future

It was that dream again, she thought numbly, clenching her bedsheets. *The point of no return.*

She had woken up from that dream every night for two weeks straight, and that hadn't been the first time she had seen it. Two years ago, when she'd first seen it, it had been so unlikely that she'd dismissed it as one of the many irrelevant futures that haunted her at night. But unlike most of those unlikely futures, this one had persisted. It had gradually become more and more likely, until it was showing up once every few weeks.

And then it had doubled in likelihood and started showing up every night.

Chronos clutched the bedsheets in angry frustration.

Two weeks ago, something had happened. That much was plain. But she couldn't see the past, and there was no way she would ask the person who could. She knew what her sister's advice would be: "Just kill the kid."

Chronos, unlike most of her family, didn't believe in killing children and teenagers. It just seemed so obviously wrong. That was why she wasn't on speaking terms with her sister. That was why she hadn't gone to her parents' funeral. That was why she basically lived like a hermit.

Well, that was a small part of the reason. The major part was that she didn't like people much.

Chronos muttered furiously under her breath and pounded the pillow beside her. She hated that dream. Hated it. Hated it. Hated it. Hated it because it was growing more likely. Hated it because it wasn't going away.

Chronos's dreams were never just dreams. They were her born mage gift acting out of control. Chronos could see the future, which wasn't the problem.

The problem was that she couldn't get it to *stop.*

Chronos closed her eyes, remembering the time she had felt cheated. The time she had learned that, if she'd just known earlier, she could have had a way to turn off her powers, if only temporarily, if only short-term.

She would have taken temporarily and short-term.

Her parents had asked her to search for futures of specific people, strangers in some sort of powerful position who could be blackmailed overseas. Her sister was the one who excelled at that, and who actually enjoyed doing it, but Chronos's parents had insisted that she should learn to do it, too.

"The two of you would be the most amazing team the family has ever known," they'd told her, "if you'd just learn to work together!"

But Chronos, who was known for her rebelliousness and uncooperativeness, had just answered rudely.

Still, because she'd had some grudging desire to please her parents, she'd put some small effort into it while grounded in her room. If nothing else, she'd had some mild curiosity about their targets, and it had turned out to be justified.

One of the targets had been a member of their greatest rival, the Deathwaves. A born mage family of great power and villainy.

And one of the target's futures had been that his seven-year-old daughter would turn into a magical girl.

Chronos lifted her fist and smashed it down into the pillow beside her. The rage she'd felt then was still strong now. She'd always been told that born mages couldn't be magical girls. That the two magic systems were natural enemies. That that was why born mages and magical girls couldn't coexist.

And it had been a lie. Everything her extended family believed in had been a lie.

Once she'd known to look for it, she'd searched for other futures like it, and there had been dozens of them. Born mage magical girl futures littered the world. Most were born mage girls with such weak powers that they didn't even realize they were born mages, yet the results were always the same. In every future, the two magic systems coexisted. More than coexisted: they could hybridize together.

In other words, if she'd had magical girl powers, she could have used them to control her born magic talent.

And it had been too late then, because she'd been too old to become one.

Two decades later, long past the point when she would have

been able to keep magical girl powers in any case, it still stang. Perhaps she would never have succeeded — it was likely, as she'd never been particularly innocent — but she had been robbed of the opportunity to try.

Chronos shook her head, reminding herself that brooding on that memory had never accomplished anything except to put her in a sour mood. The past had never gotten her anything.

The future didn't seem much better, though.

Uneasily, Chronos checked the alternate possibilities. There were hundreds of them. Thousands of them. Millions of them. All sorts of other paths the future could take. All sorts of ways the world would be safe. And yet . . .

And yet, Chronos thought, *it's getting more likely every single day.*

She knew that after that press conference, after that scene she had just witnessed, there were no futures remaining where the world would be safe. But it was three and a half years in the future. Plenty of time for something to derail it.

Except that it had been growing for two years now, and nothing had yet.

Chronos opened her fists and watched the scene she knew would happen two months after that press conference. In her hands lay a transparent landscape, a cityscape of broken buildings and a shattered moon strewn across the sky. There would normally be sound, too, but there were no sounds in this scene. There was nobody left to speak.

Chronos moved her hands and flicked back to the first scene, then flicked back further than that. Brazil's ultimatum. Cream Angel changing to Avenging Angel. Green Fairy dying.

She could do all this in her head, but she preferred to watch the images with her eyes and hear the noise with her ears. It felt more divorced from her thoughts that way. Less intrusive and unwelcomely intimate.

Their fifth arch-villain. The founding of the Magical Girl Union. Kendra deciding not to go to college. Their fourth arch-villain. Flick. Flick. Flick.

And then at last, she couldn't flick anymore. She had gone as far back as she possibly could.

That's the present, Chronos thought, touching the transparent image with her fingertips. *Or only seconds away from it.*

The fifteen-year-old girl who would destroy the world in three years lay fast asleep. She seemed so innocent and peaceful, compared to what she would one day be.

"Why?" Chronos muttered, even though she knew no one would hear her. "Why is this your future? What would cause someone to do such a thing?"

She waited, watching with narrowed eyes, but there were no answers in the present, and the past was inaccessible to her. So she flicked forward to the future, surveying tomorrow.

"Oh, so you want me to be a washed up, former magical girl whose life revolves around her glory days?" a brown-skinned girl with dozens of tiny braids was asking bitterly. "You want me to be like your *mother?*"

The fifteen-year-old Kendra leapt to her feet. "YOU TAKE THAT BACK!"

The fifteen-year-old girl with dozens of braids hopped out of her chair and headed towards the exit. "Whatever. I'm late for track."

Chronos stopped the scene and tapped her fingers on her sheets.

Trying to figure out *why* was a fool's errand. She didn't want to spend that much time watching somebody else, either. She was a hermit because she didn't want to spend time with people, and watching their futures qualified.

Unfortunately, she didn't have a choice when she was asleep.

Maybe, she thought, *maybe . . . if I stop it . . .*

Maybe then she would be able to sleep without that dream recurring constantly and driving her insane.

Her sister's methods were out of the question, of course. She'd never killed anyone, and she had no intention of starting.

But . . . Chronos thought, *a conversation . . .*

She grimaced at the thought of it. She hadn't left the apartment in two years. She paid someone to deliver groceries to her doorstep, and anything else she needed, she left a note for that person to buy it with the money.

Money had never been a problem. She'd day-traded stocks for a few weeks several years ago.

Chronos sighed heavily, and got out of bed. Unpleasant as the prospect was, she couldn't think of any other way to make the nightmares stop. Besides, the end of the world seemed like a relatively unpleasant thing.

I wonder, she thought, *could one conversation solve anything?*

Chapter 2
The Present

Kendra was bursting with pride. She'd had a fantastic idea that she could hardly wait to explain to her teammates. After last night's terrible battle, she had figured out exactly what the problem was with their team and what they needed to do to fix it. Florence might object, but she was fairly certain that she could persuade her. And Felicity . . . well, Felicity was easily persuaded by anything.

The trick would be convincing Florence. Kendra's best friend had been rather unreceptive about the same idea a year ago, but this time, Kendra was sure she could make her see the necessity.

"Hey, Flo!" Kendra called, walking briskly over and waving. She fell into step with her best friend, acting casual as if she hadn't arrived fifteen minutes early and been waiting there this whole time for her. "I wanna talk about something. About the battle last night. We have . . ."

"Shhhhhh!" Florence hissed, glancing around at the crowded hallway.

Kendra let out an exasperated sigh. "If anyone listens in, I'll erase their short-term memory. Anyway . . ."

"Or maybe you could just not say things like that at school!" Florence hissed in a strangled voice.

Kendra snorted in annoyance. Lately, not using magic had been her best friend's favorite pastime. Florence should never have joined that track team. Kendra had warned her that it would take away from their magical girl time, but no . . .

"Kendra! Florence!" an excited voice shouted. Kendra glanced over to see Felicity dashing down the hallway, brown ponytail bouncing behind her. "Wasn't that the *greatest* battle last night?"

Florence threw her hands up in the air.

"The part where I powered up because of my love for Daniel, eeeeeeeeeee!" the girl squealed, squeezing her hands into fists and jumping up and down. She made no attempt to moderate her volume. "I knew it was true love! Only true love could make me power up, right? Daniel and I are destined to be together!"

"Which is why you have the nerve to say that in public, in front of dozens of people, but you haven't yet worked up the nerve to say anything to him?" Kendra asked coolly.

Felicity's face turned red. "I — I'll tell him! I'll tell him today!"

"Would you two stop talking about these things at school?!" Florence exclaimed.

Of course, he's probably figured it out already, Kendra thought, glancing at her ditzy teammate's backpack. In permanent marker, all over it, she had written things like *Felicity + Daniel, Felicity and Daniel 4-EVER,* one great big heart with *DANIEL* in the center, and of course *Felicity Frankweiler* all over the place, which was Daniel's last name.

Really, if the boy hadn't figured it out by now, he was as clueless as Felicity, who seemed to think her stalker-crush was some sort of secret. Then again, if he *was* as clueless as Felicity, they probably belonged together, and she should get that whole "confessing her love" thing out of the way already.

Kendra was almost, sorta jealous. She hadn't had a guy she'd liked since . . . well, since their first year as magical girls. But really, she'd been busy with more important things.

Felicity giggled. "It's only been a year since our last power-up, and already I have another one!"

Florence ground her forehead into the palms of her hands.

Kendra felt a flash of irritation. It was true, Felicity had managed to power up, and she was relatively proud of her teammate and all that. But it had been a very minor power up — her focus item and costume hadn't even changed — and the battle had been horrible in every other way.

Kendra cleared her throat. "We started with an old attack that hasn't worked since our arch-minions upgraded. I wouldn't call that 'great.'"

"I got a power-up because of *Daniel!*" Felicity squealed, hugging herself.

"Would you stop saying 'power-up' at school?" Florence griped. "It's like you don't even care if —"

Kendra glanced around and saw a lot of people gathering around, watching them. She sighed and raised her arms.

"Cream Angel, *fledge!*"

She launched into the air, hovering just below the ceiling as gigantic feathered wings sprouted from her back. Now everyone in the hall was watching, but that was fine, because they wouldn't remember any of this in a minute. Kendra grabbed the golden ring of a halo off her head and spun it around her wrist.

"Cream Angel, memory erase!" she shouted.

The eyes of everybody in the hallway went glazed.

Satisfied, Kendra dropped down, detransforming at the exact moment that her feet touched the floor. She lowered her arms with effortless grace and just a hint of smugness. This was why she'd taken ballet for all those years — to learn to detransform perfectly. Magical girls who stumbled looked so uncool.

"Thank you so much," Florence hissed furiously. "That's exactly what I was hoping you would do right here in the hallway."

Kendra rolled her eyes. "Three years ago, you would have asked me to."

"Well, she did thank you," Felicity said earnestly.

The eyes of everyone around them returned to normal, and conversations and walking resumed as if nothing had ever interrupted them. Kendra waited until the student who had been listening in had walked off.

Satisfied at last that it was safe to talk again, she said, "Now, about the battle last night —"

"I powered up!" Felicity squealed.

"What part of 'secret identity' do you two not understand?" Florence asked incredulously.

"Oooooooh, what's Daniel going to say when I finally tell *him?*" Felicity squealed, hopping up and down.

"What secret identity?" Kendra snorted. "We don't shapeshift when we transform. My parents *designed* our costumes. We're officially registered with the government. If it weren't for my short-term memory eraser, the entire town would . . ."

"Yes, yes, I know, I'm very grateful that you have it," Florence said testily.

"Why don't you make a power like that yourself?" Felicity asked helpfully, bouncing up and down. "Next time you power up?"

"Oh, because that's so easy," Florence said in an undertone, glancing around the hall with a paranoid eye.

Felicity giggled. "You just have to fall in love again, and —"

"We'll talk about that later!" Kendra broke in, anticipating the firestorm of her friend's rage if the ditz finished that sentence. Florence's last relationship had ended very, very badly. As in, "the guy had turned out to be a villain in disguise" badly.

Sure enough, Florence looked very grumpy. "If you tell the rest of the track team I spend my weekends dressed like a cheerleader, you're dead," she muttered.

This was a safer subject, and besides, it was a silly objection. Kendra's parents had designed their costumes, but Florence herself had insisted on fluffy pink. "You didn't mind your costume three years ago —" Kendra began.

"Three years ago, I was twelve," Florence cut in. "Besides, that was before we developed 'frills of justice.' What, would you rather I acted like Felicity?"

"Gasp!" Felicity shouted. She didn't gasp — she said the word out loud. "If I saved Daniel from a minion sometime, do you think he'd fall in love with my magical girl form?"

"*Again!*" Florence cried. "Secret —!"

"Oh no!" Felicity howled and burst into sobs. "If that happened, that would create a love triangle, and he'd never look at *normal* me again!"

Chronos loitered outside the building, waiting for the school bell to ring. She knew that it would happen in eighteen seconds, so she counted down the seconds impatiently.

The idea of school bells seemed foreign to her, though she had seen them in many other people's futures. She had never been to any sort of school; her family had had its own way of doing things, and that way had not included letting governments know their children existed.

Chronos had grown up her whole life being told about the terrible anti-born mage discrimination laws, and the fact that ordinary humans would hate her for being superior if they knew about her.

Most of her family's work during her childhood had involved blackmailing and bribing politicians of the Greek government to have those laws repealed. They had succeeded so well that Greece was now infamous as a haven for villains.

The bell rang, and Chronos glanced down at her watch, although she didn't need to be told that it was 3:15. The futures were swirling and settling now. The future Avenging Angel would walk out the door in one minute . . . no, three . . . no, two . . .

Doors burst open and students poured out. Chronos flinched and reeled back as the futures assaulted her.

There was a popular girl kissing three different boys during the same night. The glimpses at first seemed like three separate futures, but they weren't. Busy girl. There was a shy freckled teenager whose unlikely futures included dying in a car accident and becoming a singing magical girl. Four boys from the basketball team walked past, likely to win the state championship. A surly grumpy girl walked past, and Chronos saw her squealing with joy over her cat.

The Present

Dozens of futures. Hundreds of futures. All of them irrelevant.
All of them unwanted. *Bam. Bam. Bam. Bam.* It had been so long
since Chronos had had to deal with a crowd, she was overwhelmed.
She closed her eyes and clutched her head, and —

A flash of the Wings of Justice appeared.

Chronos's eyes flew open. Now coming out of the door were
Kendra and her two teammates. They seemed to be deep in an
argument.

"You want me to miss track for . . . *combat practice?*" the
dark-skinned girl with dozens of tiny braids demanded.

"Did you see? Daniel *looked* at me in fourth period!" the
pale-skinned girl with a brown ponytail squealed, bouncing up
and down as she walked.

Crimson Dragon and Green Fairy, Chronos identified them.
She checked their futures to confirm that, and corrected herself.
*Pink Dragon. The one with the braids hasn't changed her magical girl
form yet.*

"You can't deny we desperately need it," the blonde-haired
Kendra announced, looking straight at the girl with the braids
and ignoring the other one. "If we're ever going to power up
again, we need to learn the meaning of teamwork —"

"I'm going to learn the meaning of teamwork in *track,*" the
other girl said, starting to march away.

Kendra seized her by the end of a handful of braids. "No,
you're not. This is important —"

"Felicity and Daniel, sittin' in a tree!" the other girl burst out
singing, oblivious to her friends' disagreement. "K-I-S-S-I-N-G!
First comes love, then comes . . ."

She stopped, finally seeming to notice her friends' heavy glares.

"What?" she asked, blinking.

It took a lot of effort to pry Florence away from her precious
track practice, so Kendra was relieved when they finally entered
the ice cream parlor.

"Okay, here's the deal," Kendra said, sitting down at the nearest table. She tried to ignore the fact that Felicity, who had insisted that they hold the meeting here, was now flipping through the menu with avid enthusiasm rather than listening. "We haven't had an arch-nemesis since we defeated Queen Hemlock, and I think that's made us go soft."

"I hope you're not suggesting we pick a fight with someone new," Florence said sourly. "Isn't saving the world three times enough?"

"Of course it's not!" Kendra snapped. "We still have power, hence responsibility! Besides, what's with this attitude? Wings of Justice was *your* idea!"

"Does anybody want to buy me ice cream?" Felicity's voice poked in.

"Well, no one said I'd have to stay Pink Dragon for the rest of my *life*," Florence said angrily.

"Adults can't become magical girls!" Kendra snapped. "You won't be *doing* this the rest of your life! That's why it's all the more important to put all of your time and effort and emotional investment into this *now!*"

"Doesn't anybody want to buy me ice cream?" Felicity's voice asked tearfully.

"Oh, so you want me to be a washed up, former magical girl whose life revolves around her glory days?" Florence asked bitterly. "You want me to be like your *mother?*"

Kendra leapt to her feet in outrage. "YOU TAKE THAT BACK!"

Florence hopped up out of her chair and headed for the exit. "Whatever. I'm late for track."

"*Florence!*" Kendra shouted.

But the door swung shut, and Florence was gone.

Kendra sat down, her fists clenching and unclenching in fury. She admired her mother. She wanted to emulate her mother. Her mother had kept her magical girl powers until nineteen years old, even though most girls outgrew them between sixteen to eighteen. Kendra's mother had been so innocent, so pure, so good that the magic had still wanted her even that late. Even now, her mother spoke about magic with reverence and regret.

The Present

Kendra had always known that she would one day be a magical girl. And she had always known that she would be so good, so pure, so righteous that the magic would choose her to stay a wielder of it past high school age. Just like her mother had.

She'd based her whole childhood around that. She could have become a magical girl much earlier, but she had chosen to wait until she was twelve, so that she felt ready to do it *right*. She'd studied magical girls through history. She'd taken ballet and martial arts classes. She'd even learned German, the language of the world's first magical girl, so that she could read books about Sönnig in her original language.

The only thing that had derailed her plans had been Florence, her best friend, who had insisted that if Kendra was going to become a magical girl, she wanted to be one, too. And, not content with that, she'd wanted to be a team.

Kendra's jaw clenched. *So I based my magical girl form around being part of a team. I can't change my powers to be an effective solo magical girl unless I power up — and it would be very difficult to do that without her.*

How could Florence, who was supposed to be her best friend, be so selfish? She'd insisted on shoving her way into this part of Kendra's life. Now she couldn't just slack off or leave or quit.

Kendra came back to herself and realized Felicity was yammering something about Daniel and yearbook photography.

"I'll let you obsess in peace," Kendra said, shoving her chair back and standing.

"Hey, why are you leaving?" Felicity asked blankly, looking around. "Where'd Florence go?"

Why did we ever let her win the audition to join our team? Kendra wondered, marching out of the building.

Chapter 3
The Vision

Marching down the sidewalk, Kendra continued fuming. *"Pick a fight with someone new," she said . . . and I* don't *pick fights! The FBI assigned us to the drug lord, and Queen Hemlock and Dark Deathzone attacked us* first!

Okay, granted, Dark Deathzone was a minion of our first villain, and we started the fight with Dark Deathwave when we mistook him for Dark Deathzone . . . but that's not the same thing!

Villains really needed to learn to use more original names.

If she'd just listened, Kendra thought, frustrated, *she would have seen that I had a terrific idea. This is just like that time we lost the Magical Girl Team of the Year competition to stupid Victory's Bloom!*

Kendra still blamed her best friend for that. Florence had insisted that they use a team pose Kendra had known looked lame, and sure enough, they'd placed *sixth*. Meanwhile, the winning team had completely imploded on stage when one of the girls had accused the team leader of hogging all the power-ups and never letting the other two do anything useful in battle.

I mean, really! Kendra thought. *Our magical girl forms even looked cooler! And who names their magical girl form "Geranium," anyway?!* It had been two years since they'd failed to win the competition, but the memory still rankled.

But Kendra was too mad about her current grievances to focus too long on an old one. Was it too much to ask that Florence be in a good mood so that she could persuade her to let their team volunteer as FBI aides again?

I don't even know why she made us quit in the first place! Kendra thought indignantly. *Well . . . okay, I do know.* Florence had gotten really mad when Kendra had killed their first assigned arch-nemesis instead of capturing him so that he could stand trial. But seriously, the guy had bribed two judges and gotten off scot-free twice already. What other way would there have been to stop the problem?

She'd claimed it was unethical to kill someone when you could have captured them. And sure, Kendra had worried about that, too. But their handler at the FBI had explained to her that magical girls weren't bound by the same regulations as law enforcement officers, and that as long as her magic continued to think she was worthy, she could take that as a sign that she was doing okay. That was even one of the reasons magical girl aides were so helpful to law enforcement, he had explained.

But when Kendra had passed along this wisdom to Florence, she'd blown her top. She'd said that if they didn't quit helping the FBI, she'd quit the team.

But that was two and a half years ago, Kendra would have insisted. *We'd have a different handler this time, and anyway, there are some regulations about magical girl aides now.*

She probably would have even managed to keep from adding, "Unfortunately."

So really, how *dare* Florence not listen to her? This was something they needed to do, as a team! Otherwise they'd keep stagnating!

Kendra became aware that someone was following her.

Without a pause in her stride, without stopping to think, she threw her arms in the air and shouted, "Cream Angel . . . *fledge!*"

Her body soared up into the air, and Kendra danced and flipped through the acrobats she had choreographed for her transformation scene.

She'd tried to choreograph awesome ones for her teammates, as well, but noooo, they had refused to use them. "That looks too difficult," Felicity had complained, and Florence had said, "If you think I'm doing anything but hiding while my clothes disappear, you're dead wrong."

Really, Kendra thought, grabbing her halo from the air as it appeared over her head, *it's like they're missing the whole point of transforming. It's not like anyone's supposed to* watch *you. You're just supposed to look cool!*

The last of her angelic robes appeared and shot upwards into a double-layered short skirt, and a red sash came from nowhere and tied itself around her waist. Kendra spread her fingers like the wings of a bird of prey, and dove down at the villain who had been behind her.

The target tried to leap aside, but Kendra was too quick. She jabbed her halo against the villain's throat.

"*Speak, villain!*" she shouted. "Why were you following me?"

"I just wanted to talk to you!" the villain exclaimed.

Kendra narrowed her eyes. "All right. Talk."

"Well, first of all, I'm not a villain!" the villain said furiously.

Kendra snorted, but her arm didn't waver. "I grant that you look more like a hobo, but that's just a disguise."

"I do not!" the villain exclaimed. "I brushed and washed my hair, and I'm wearing a skirt! It isn't even dirty!"

Kendra wrinkled her nose, her arm still unwavering. "Well, it smells like something."

"Mothballs!" the hobo shouted. "That's the smell of mothballs!"

Kendra shrugged with the shoulder that was not holding the halo. "All right. Then who or what are you?"

"My name is Chronos," the hobo said. "I'm a born mage."

Kendra snorted. "Which almost certainly makes you a villain."

"It does not!" the hobo shouted. "Put that halo away!"

"I think I'll hang on to it, thanks," Kendra said dryly. "Why were you following me?"

The hobo straightened, and seemed to be making an attempt to sound mysterious. "Because of my power. I can see the future."

Kendra burst out laughing, her arm holding the halo falling to her side as she clutched her stomach. This ludicrous hobo, with the power of an arch-villain? Oh, yeah, right!

"It's the truth!" the woman shouted.

Snapping her halo back into threatening position and wiping a tear away from her eye, Kendra jeered, "All right, soothsayer. If you're so smart, prove it."

The woman looked annoyed. "I didn't say I was *smart*; I said I could see the *future.*"

It was all Kendra could do to keep from laughing again. She'd seen carnival fortune tellers claiming that they had magical powers before, and those claims were beyond ludicrous. They were too old to be magical girls, and too drab to be born mages, a.k.a. villains.

"Uh huh," Kendra smirked. "Why don't you just . . ."

"And you'll want to stop that child from running into the street," the woman added, pointing over her shoulder.

Kendra spun around and saw a small child running after a ball that was bouncing straight at the road.

Kendra's wings flared as she shot forward and grabbed the girl and ball right before they hit the street. A second later, a car raced around the bend three times faster than it should have been going, right where the girl would have been.

Kendra's heart beat wildly as she set the kid down and the kid ran off towards a sandbox. There were parents everywhere, seeing as she had been walking right beside a playground, but somehow, no one had noticed that the kid had run off.

Was it possible . . . was it feasible . . . that the hobo *could* see the future?

Or had the whole demonstration just been staged?

Kendra couldn't decide. The two seemed equally likely.

"So," the hobo said from a seated position. She was sitting on the sidewalk, despite the fact that it was filthy and covered with sand. "Do you believe me?"

"Maybe . . ." Kendra said cautiously.

"What would convince you?" the woman asked.

"An explanation wouldn't hurt," Kendra said darkly. "Why were you following me?"

The born mage hobo shrugged. "I figured it was high time someone told you not all magical girls are inherently good."

"*What?!*" Kendra shouted.

"You heard me."

"That's *absurd!*" Kendra burst out, shoving her arms outward. "*Everyone* knows our magic only works for the pure in heart!"

"Yes, I've heard the propaganda," the woman said coolly. "It's true a girl has to be young, innocent, and well-intentioned to become a magical girl. But I've studied the magic system since before you were born. After gaining their powers, magical girls *can* become corrupt."

Oh, *that* was what she was talking about. Kendra relaxed microscopically.

"Well, sure, but then they'll lose their powers," she said, as if speaking to an idiot. Her halo spun in the air over her hand. "Just as if they'd grown too old or given them up willingly —"

"— or died," the hobo finished for her. "But, Kendra, I think you're missing something. Only death or voluntary loss make magical girls powers vanish instantly."

Kendra didn't ask how the hobo knew her name. It wasn't the first time a villain had figured out her secret identity. She'd never gone to much effort to keep it hidden.

"Don't be dumb," Kendra said impatiently. "I've seen recordings of defectors. Their focus items crumble, and they lose their transformations permanently!"

I mean, really, you couldn't get much more instant than that. The second a magical girl declared that she was turning to villainy, all her powers and costume and transformation vanished immediately. And it wasn't just defectors, either. When a magical girl quit for any other reason, the results were the same.

"There *are* dark magical girls," Kendra conceded. "Is that what you mean? But they're brainwashed by villains. When you take away the magic brainwashing them, they go back to normal again. They're still pure underneath."

The hobo brushed away this comment as if it were irrelevant. "Well, obviously. But I meant real magical girls. Like you. The kind who look completely harmless on the surface."

Kendra bristled. If there was one thing she did not consider herself, it was *harmless*. She was mighty and powerful. She was a strong force for good.

"You say you've seen recordings of defectors," the hobo said. "It's true that the news loves to report those rare events. It looks so convincing, doesn't it? The instant a girl decides to turn evil, she loses her magic permanently."

"Right," Kendra said, nodding sharply. She was starting to feel irritated.

"Think it through, Kendra," the hobo said. "A girl declares her intention to join the other side, then loses all her magic. The same thing happens with all defectors. But that isn't because they've just turned evil. It's because they're choosing to give up their magical girl forms *after* turning evil. Do you really think that anyone would make such a decision out of nowhere? In a split second? Do you really think those people change drastically overnight?"

Kendra was starting to see red. "MAGICAL GIRLS DON'T TURN EVIL!"

". . . And yet you assume all born mages do," the hobo said. "Why are you so quick to judge my people, and so quick to praise yours? Haven't you ever heard the saying, 'Power corrupts; absolute power corrupts absolutely'?"

"I wrote a paper on how that *doesn't* apply to magical girls in fourth grade," Kendra snapped.

The hobo looked unsurprised, then exasperated.

"Look, it's been nice chatting," Kendra said, starting to walk off, "but I have combat practice to salvage, a best friend to chew out, and —"

"I didn't come without proof, Kendra!" the woman interrupted. "Would you like to see it?"

Kendra hesitated.

Proof?

"All right," Kendra said slowly, turning around.

The hobo held a hand out, cupping it, and images appeared. A pair of wings; a whip; a halo. Then a full scene appeared, tiny in the palm of her hand. The woman pinched it, and it stretched out wide before them. Sound began to swell from it, too.

"— to protect world peace!" a politician was shouting from a podium.

"World peace! World peace! World peace!" a crowd shouted. "World peace! World peace! World peace!"

The woman pulled the image, and it zoomed forward to another scene. The same politician, zooming through the air with a mob of flying magical girls behind her. Her flowing robes were bloodred, as were her wings.

"That looks like Mágico," Kendra commented. "That's the style of magical girl outfit they wear out there. Is this from the revolution?"

The born mage hobo said nothing, and the scene changed.

Now there was a terrible battle. Very little bloodshed, since most magical girl powers didn't shed blood and most magical girl forms didn't bleed, but there were thousands dying. One girl engulfed a soldier in what looked like cotton candy, then another soldier launched at her and mowed her down with bullets. She fell to the ground, detransforming, and he shot the bullets through her again, killing her human life as well.

"What in the world?!" Kendra screamed. "You don't *do* that! Killing a magical girl form, that I can get, but you don't kill someone *permanently!*"

The born mage's eyes hardened, and she changed scenes.

"If you see a kid on the battlefield, do *not* let it live!" an enemy commander was shouting. "I don't care if you know you killed its magical form! The younger they are, the more likely they are to get magic all over again! And those things *aren't* innocent! They mean to destroy our entire country!"

"Moron," Kendra muttered. "It's true that younger girls don't have to be as pure as older ones, but there's still a minimum level. If they're attacking you, you clearly deserved it."

"But they're kids," a subordinate objected. "We can't kill kids —"

The superior's fist thumped down. "They're killing *us,* aren't they? *We* don't have a spare life we can just throw away!"

"Nobody throws a magical girl life away," Kendra said, riled. "There's no guarantee that you could become a magical girl again. The vast majority of girls who die as magical girls don't!"

The scene dissolved, and a new one took its place.

"Kill the hostages," the woman with the bloodred robes said, stretching out her hand.

"But they're innocent!" a girl with an Australian accent protested. She was dressed much like a figure skater, and wore ice skates. "We can't do that!"

"We said we would if they didn't release our allies, didn't we?" the woman snapped. "We'll lose all credibility if we don't follow through on our threats."

"I told you not to make that threat, didn't I?" an Asian girl said coolly. She wore what looked like a kimono and had flowers drifting lazily through her hair. "It didn't work well against Emperor Kami, and it won't work well here."

"Thank you for your opinion, Namikaze," the woman snapped. "But I remind you that we still overthrew the man."

Oh. Kendra's mouth opened. She'd been thinking she was watching scenes from the Mágico revolution, when magical girls had freed a portion of Brazil from the tyranny of its dictator who had persecuted magical girls, but now she realized she wasn't. Emperor Kami was still on the throne of Japan.

Which means . . . Kendra thought. *Which means . . . this is the future?*

That would make more sense. The woman had said she could see the future. Maybe she could show it, as well. It was a fascinating power, one that Kendra would have found extremely admirable if it had belonged to a magical girl, but unfortunately, being from a born mage, that made it suspicious. It could very well be an illusion power, for instance. Everything she was watching could be fiction.

But there's something . . . Kendra thought, unsettled. *There's something that seems . . . familiar . . .*

No. Kendra shook her head. She'd never seen that woman before. What was familiar was the costume, which was rather like one she had been designing for her next power-up. She'd already planned out Florence's, which would be that color of bloodred, so that she'd stop complaining about her costume being pink.

Maybe not that shade, after all, Kendra thought, *if there's a villain masquerading as a magical girl who dresses like that.*

Because that was clearly what was going on here. If those future scenes she was currently seeing were real, it was a villain who had infiltrated the whole magical girl community and made them think she was one of them. Kendra wasn't sure how, since magical girls were the only ones with magic that allowed for transformation, but perhaps a tricky villain from another world could pretend they did through illusion magic.

The only question, Kendra thought, watching the woman kill off the hostages herself, *is, why did this hobo come to me?*

As she watched the army of magical girls overrun the world, shattering cities, the answer became clear.

Because we're the only ones who can stop it. We're the ones who are meant to save the world from that charlatan monster. Even a born mage doesn't want to see the world ruled and destroyed by somebody from another world, and if she sees the future, she knows we need this information so that we can stop her.

The moon exploded in the born mage's hands, scattering fragments across the sky. A terrible earthquake roared.

Of course, Kendra thought, nodding. She had never failed to do what was necessary, no matter what the cost. She would do whatever she had to to protect world peace.

"Do you understand?" the born mage asked softly, as devastation continued spreading within her hands.

Yes, Kendra tried to answer, but she couldn't manage to speak. The magnitude of the disaster was too big to take in. The responsibility to stop it was too tremendous. But she mustn't let fear stand in her way. The world needed her.

Kendra licked her lips and swallowed to allow her dry throat to recover. "Is that . . . our new arch-nemesis?" she managed.

For a moment, the visions ceased. The hobo was staring at her with what looked like pity. Then the born mage twitched her fingers, and a new scene appeared. Florence was there.

Kendra recognized her in an instant. She had the same face, the same braids, and a new costume that looked nothing like Kendra had designed for her friend's next power-up — typical Florence.

The woman in the bloodred wings was standing there, too, with her back to Florence.

This is the part where we defeat her, Kendra thought. *Or — no. Is the hobo warning me that Florence is going to die in the attempt?*

Her heart squeezed at the thought. It was an awful idea. If Florence was going to die, then she should let her friend quit. Kendra could save the world by herself if she had to.

But then the woman turned around, and she looked very, very familiar. The way she'd held her face before, such rage and fury, had seemed clearly villainish. But the way she looked at Florence now was different.

The woman's face now looked familiar.

Horrifyingly familiar.

"Kendra, you can't take civilians hostage!" the future Florence said angrily. "If you do that, you'll be crossing the line!"

"They keep on killing our allies," the other woman snapped. "Not just their magical girl forms, but their human lives. They won't negotiate. They won't stop. We have to do whatever's necessary to save more lives."

"But their families are innocent!" the future Florence cried.

"And so are our allies," the woman said quietly. "I won't have to make good on our threat. It won't come to that. But I have to make it if we want those girls to come home alive."

"But even *threatening* —"

"Do you want our allies returned, or not?" the woman roared in fury.

The scene waited, and the born mage waited silently.

"So . . . so our arch-nemesis looks like that," Kendra said shakily. "She even has Florence fooled. Is . . . is that a doppelganger?"

In answer, the born mage lifted her hands.

"We will do whatever is necessary," a translucent image of Kendra as she was now said, "to protect world peace."

Yelling at Florence. "To protect world peace!"

Standing before the FBI branch office. "To protect world peace."

Speaking at their high school graduation. "To protect world peace . . ."

Standing over a dead Felicity. "To protect world peace!"

Now in the bloodred costume. "To protect world peace."

Founding the Magical Girl Union. "To protect world peace!"

Leading the mob of magical girls following her into the horrible, bloodless battlefield. "World peace! World peace! World peace!"

There was silence as the images faded and the born mage lowered her arms.

"No," she said. "I wish it were."

"That's not me!" Kendra screamed. "That *can't* be me!"

"I can show you five complete paths from now to then," the born mage said. "It's rapidly becoming your most likely future."

"NO! YOU'RE LYING! I'D NEVER TURN EVIL! *NEVER!!*" Kendra screamed.

Around her she felt feathers flying. She realized dimly that she must be detransforming. It was as if part of her wanted to shove the magic away. As if doing so would make the whole future dissolve and vanish.

"Fine. Ignore my warning," the hobo said coldly. "Your choice."

"But . . . but I wouldn't," Kendra murmured, stumbling over the words. She was too stunned and lost to make any coherent argument. "I'm *good.*"

"And let's hope you stay that way," the woman said, shoving the bloodred-woman future into her face.

Kendra burst into tears.

Did I go too far? Chronos wondered, unsure of herself. She never knew how to talk to people. She hadn't meant to make anyone cry.

On the other hand . . . wasn't that a good thing? If this conversation made a strong impression, maybe it would stop that future. Maybe it would end it permanently. Chronos had no way to know; she couldn't see any futures that she herself was in, and right now, this girl's future was clearly dependent on their conversation.

Clearly, because it was in flux, and almost all of the girl's futures were now invisible to her.

What can I do? Chronos wondered. *What should I do?*

She knew what she wanted to do. She wanted to just walk away. She'd gotten here by teleporter, a magical device her uncle had made, so it would take no time at all to get right back home and resume ignoring the problem, like she'd wanted to do in the first place.

But . . .

But what if she's not convinced? Chronos wondered. *What if I only made things worse? What if I made her more determined, and it makes everything happen sooner?*

That was a risk she didn't want to take. She wanted the future resolved. She wanted the nightmares over. She wanted to go home and know that she'd never have to return again. She had to make sure that future was gone *now.*

"The thing about evil magical girls," Chronos said, "is that most times corruption is a gradual process. The magic system's too merciful. Magical girls don't lose their powers when they start going corrupt — they lose their powers when they finish. Which is why evil magical girls are possi—"

"MAGICAL GIRLS DON'T TURN EVIL!!" Kendra screamed, leaping to her feet.

Chronos was about to snap back, but then realized that the girl was teetering on her feet, her eyes wild, looking unstable.

"Except for the rare cases that do," Chronos said gently.

The girl burst into tears again and collapsed back on the ground.

Is that . . . it? Chronos wondered, unsettled. *Can I go now?*

She felt guilty to have caused such devastation, but she didn't know how to fix it. She didn't know if comfort would help the future or hurt it. Besides, she didn't know what comfort would be possible. She wasn't going to lie to be reassuring.

Maybe she should go now. Yes, that was the best thing she could do. Chronos pulled the teleporting watch her uncle had given her out of her pocket —

She stopped.

Maybe the problem was that Kendra felt trapped. Trapped in a future she couldn't escape. Trapped without hope or possibilities.

Chronos knew how it felt to be trapped.

That was why her uncle had given her this watch.

"Teleportation represents freedom," he'd said. *"You can go anywhere, do anything, and nobody can stop you."*

As a child, that had meant a lot to her. It had meant hiding from her older sister. It had meant avoiding the head of the family. It had meant escaping from the entire villain lifestyle when she'd been old enough to take care of herself.

Perhaps, to a corrupt magical girl, it would mean starting a fresh life somewhere new.

Chronos took a deep breath, and then placed the watch on the ground beside the sobbing magical girl. This had been her childhood treasure, but she no longer needed it.

"Here," Chronos said. "My uncle made this for me when I was down one day. It teleports. It's useful." She hesitated. "I'll book a flight home."

A crowd had gathered at some point to watch them, and Chronos used her elbows to shove people aside as she walked briskly down the sidewalk. She felt naked without the watch, without a way to escape, but nobody challenged her.

She'd have to book a flight with the Deathwaves, of course, because she had no legal passport and had never bothered purchasing a fake one. But that would be easy to enough to do. It took her only a few seconds to find the future of a random Deathwave minion and to follow it to the nearest office.

Chronos turned a corner, away from the crowd, and breathed a sigh of relief. She headed toward the Deathwaves' office.

She had a long flight home back to Greece. She wasn't looking forward to it.

Chapter 4
The Decision

A crowd of people gathered around Kendra, and some of them started asking her if something was wrong.

Are you kidding me? Kendra thought furiously. *Leave me alone! Why don't you go chase after the born mage, if you're so worried?*

But then she realized that the born mage hadn't looked anything like a villain. She'd looked like a hobo. And Kendra had transformed. As far as the crowd was concerned, all the magic had been hers.

For some reason, this realization left Kendra feeling even more depressed than she had been before.

My magic failed to warn me that I was doing anything wrong, she thought. *Instead, a born mage had to. A* born mage *had to.*

Everyone knew born mages were evil. If a *born mage* had needed to stop her, she'd been destined to become a nightmare indeed.

Forget being the hero, Kendra thought bitterly, *I'm not even better than a villain.*

She wished she could believe the born mage had been lying, but that just didn't fit. Too many of the details had meshed with Kendra's own plans for the future, including ones she'd never written down or told anybody.

The bloodred woman's hairstyle.

Her costume's shape.

The Magical Girl Union.

Well, to be fair, Kendra had joked with Florence about the need for magical girls to have their own governing body. Only magical girls could fairly judge magical girls, after all. But she had never said she'd been *serious*.

Unless the born mage was a mind-reader, she doubted that all of those details could have come out.

For a moment, Kendra's heart lifted at the possibility. Born mages only ever had one power, so mind-reading and illusion couldn't happen in one person, but what if there had been a second born mage involved?

This could just be a plot to convince her to quit her powers, right before the world needed her. Kendra brightened at the idea. That was it. She'd just been lied to. It was going to be fine. The world still needed her.

That thought sustained her enough to stand up, to inform the crowd briskly that she was fine, and to start walking home.

But as she headed down the sidewalk, alone now, her pace flagged. Her shoulders grew tighter and tighter.

The problem was . . . the problem was, there was one simple fact she couldn't explain like that, and that was a common sense point the hobo had made.

"Do you really think those people change drastically overnight?"

If magical girls could be evil . . . if they could turn corrupt gradually and still have their powers until the process was complete . . .

Well, then it made perfect sense that Kendra might be one of them.

Kendra's pace slowed to a dead stop. Despair washed over her.

She wasn't like Florence. She didn't have a moral compass born from a religion. She based her moral compass on what she had been told, and on believing that the magic system would stop her if she ever went corrupt. Therefore, whenever she'd done something questionable and Florence had called her on it, she'd known that she was right and Florence was wrong.

For instance, choosing to kill their first arch-nemesis instead of taking him prisoner.

Tears squeezed out of Kendra's eyes.

The Decision

It wasn't fair. She'd always followed what she had been told.
She's always believed what she had been told. And everybody had
let her down. *Magic* had let her down.

And that was when Kendra realized . . .

No. Magic didn't fail me. I failed magic.

Kendra drew in a shaky breath, trying not to bawl again. Yes.
She had failed magic. She didn't deserve it anymore.

But she couldn't bear to give it up.

Please, Kendra pleaded silently, *isn't there any way I can keep it?*

All she wanted to do was save the world. All she wanted to be
was a hero. Giving up couldn't be the answer to that. It couldn't.

But she had only two sure ways to make sure that future
didn't happen, and she would never consider suicide. That was a
coward's way out. Which meant that the only real option to make
sure that, no matter how tempted she got in the future, she
would never become that person was . . .

If I gave up my powers . . .

Kendra shivered, and forced herself to continue walking
down the sidewalk back home.

She wasn't ready to stop being a magical girl. She wasn't *done*.
She'd never intended to quit; she'd intended to keep her powers
for as long as possible until magic itself abandoned her for being
too old.

She'd always said she'd do the right thing, no matter what
the cost. But this was not a cost she had anticipated. This was
not a cost she had been willing to pay.

But if it was the right thing . . .

Kendra stopped again as another thought struck her.

Is it the right thing?

Because there was another logical conclusion to draw from
what she had just learned.

"The world *does* need me to save it," Kendra murmured.
"I see . . ."

Florence was getting really worried. Somebody had called her after track practice to say he'd seen Kendra crying in the park. Then Florence had called Kendra's house, and her parents had said she'd been refusing to speak to anybody. And now Kendra had skipped school all day.

We've fought before, Florence thought uneasily. *A lot. Kendra's never cried about it. What's made this time so different?*

She and Kendra had always had a . . . dynamic friendship. Even as kids, they'd gone from best friends to worst enemies to best friends many times in a week. They'd been fighting more than usual lately, but that was just because Florence had been wondering whether she wanted to stay a magical girl at all, and Kendra'd had strong opinions about the matter and problems with the whole "staying out of other people's business" thing.

But something must have been different this time. Florence must have really hurt her best friend. And she had no clue what she'd said.

She caught up to Felicity near the bleachers after she'd finished running a few laps on the track. "Any sign of Kendra?" Florence panted, pulling a handful of braids off her sweaty neck.

Felicity shook her head. Her eyes brightened. "But I gave Daniel my phone number!"

"Really?" Florence was startled. "You told him you like him?"

Felicity giggled, turning red. "No, no! I wrote it on his backpack while he wasn't looking!"

"Well, then I'm sure he'll know exactly what that means and what to do about it," Florence said, rolling her eyes.

"Kendra!" Felicity gasped, pointing behind Florence.

Florence spun around, and there was a slumped figure, standing with a wall of blonde hair covering her face.

"Kendra . . .?" Florence asked uneasily.

"Where did you come from?!" Felicity exclaimed. "You just, like, appeared out of nowhere! Where have you *been?*"

"Do I want to know why you skipped school?" Florence added in an accusing tone, hoping to provoke a reaction.

Kendra said nothing.

The Decision

Florence felt a stab of uncertainty. What was wrong with Kendra? She never acted like this. She always had something to say, often some kind of order that drove Florence crazy.

Did I jump to the wrong conclusions yesterday? Florence wondered. *I thought she was going to pester us to apply as FBI aides yet again. Maybe she wasn't. Maybe she wanted to suggest that we become singing magical girls or something.*

The more she thought about it, the more likely it seemed. Kendra's mother had been a singing magical girl, and Kendra really admired her. Kendra also knew that Florence's favorite musician was a singing magical girl in South Africa, and she knew that Felicity loved singing along to songs on the radio.

Badly and out of tune. But most singing magical girls had autotune magic, so that wouldn't be a big deal.

If that was the case, Florence felt awful for ignoring her. She'd assumed that Kendra was still obsessed with that whole "saving the world" schtick, but maybe she wasn't. Maybe Kendra had been trying to be unselfish, for once, and Florence had thrown it in her face.

"Kendra?" Florence asked cautiously.

Kendra finally spoke, but she did not raise her head. Her long, blonde hair was like a wall between them. "I've been up all night, thinking. And I think . . . we need to split up our team."

"*WHAT?!*" Felicity shrieked. Loose hair clips from her ponytail went flying all over the place. She'd worn about three dozen of them today, and she'd been losing them all day.

"Well, *that's* a complete 180 . . ." Florence muttered, with a flash of irritation.

She couldn't believe she'd been so worried. Kendra was just being Kendra, it seemed. She'd high-handedly decided to fire them both from Wings of Justice without their permission.

"I'm sorry if I've talked too much about Daniel . . ." Felicity sobbed, burying her face in her hands.

"Who do you want to train to take our place?" Florence asked, almost as accusingly as she'd intended.

"No," Kendra said. "That's not what I meant at all."

Florence noticed for the first time that Kendra was holding her halo. That was odd, because your focus item didn't do anything unless you were transformed. You could summon it whenever, but there was no real point in doing so.

As Kendra spoke, a flutter of feathers surrounded her halo — not Kendra herself, which was even odder, because they would normally be part of her transformation scene.

"I've decided," Kendra said quietly, "to become . . . a villain instead."

Florence's mouth fell open as the halo grew spikes. Thick iron spikes jabbed out of the gold ring.

"*WHAT?!*" she burst out, hearing Felicity say the same.

Kendra raised her head at last, and there were tears in her eyes. "If magical girls can betray the world, then someone has to stop them! So as of right now, I'm officially defecting!"

"Are you insane?" Florence yelped.

"Teleport!" Kendra screamed, raising the spiked halo and something else in her other hand over her head. Then, with a poof of sparkles, she was gone.

Florence stared at the empty air, unable to fathom what she had just witnessed. Kendra had said she was . . . defecting?

Kendra?

Kendra, of all people?

That didn't even make sense! Defectors lost their powers, and their focus items crumbled! Kendra's focus item had grown spikes, as if it had become a villain weapon instead!

"What just happened?" Florence burst out, trying to process it.

"I wanna wake up from this dreeeam!" Felicity wailed.

What the —? Florence thought. *WHAT?!*

Chronos settled in with a book she'd read many times. She was glad to get back to her routine of doing not much of anything. She hadn't had any nightmares on the plane home, which hopefully meant that she could go back to ignoring everybody.

"Hm?" A twinkle of light caught the corner of her eye, and she turned around, wondering idly what —

"*Kendra?*"

The corrupt magical girl was standing there, spiked ring in one hand and watch in the other, glowering fiercely.

"Um . . ." Chronos said. "I think you took a wrong turn —"

"I defected," the magical girl said darkly. "Now I can never wreck the world, and no one can ever wreck the world in my name. But that doesn't solve the problem permanently, does it?"

What are you talking about? Chronos stared at her, baffled. *That solves the problem entirely. Granted, you could just have quit your magic, and I'm not sure why you didn't, but . . .*

"If I was going to turn evil, I won't be the last one," Kendra explained sharply. "So you're going to help me fight the corrupt. We'll form a villain team."

"WHAT?" Chronos exploded. "I don't do teams! And I'm not a villain — I'm *neutral!*"

"Not anymore," the magical girl said. "You want to save the world? Help me stop the people who threaten it."

"I *don't* want to save the world!" Chronos protested. "I just wanted to end my nightmares about *you!*"

"Congratulations," Kendra said, spinning on her heel and walking towards the door. "Where's your guest room?"

"You're *not staying!*" Chronos shouted. "Leave me *alone!*"

"Too late for that, oracle."

"The name's 'Chronos' —"

"Whatever you say, soothsayer."

"CHRONOS!"